Dirty Bertie

UNDERPANTS!

For Lynsey and Paul ~ D R

For Philip, old friendships are the best ~ A M

STRIPES PUBLISHING
An imprint of Magi Publications
1 The Coda Centre, 189 Munster Road,
London SW6 6AW

A paperback original
First published in Great Britain in 2007
This edition published 2011

Characters created by David Roberts
Text copyright © Alan MacDonald, 2007
Illustrations copyright © David Roberts, 2007

ISBN: 978-1-84715-222-0

Printed and bound in China.
STP/1800/0010/0911
10 9 8 7 6 5 4 3 2 1

Dirty Bertie

UNDERPANTS!

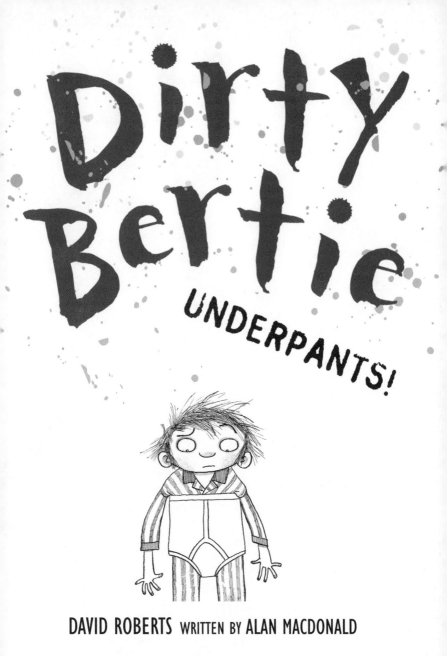

DAVID ROBERTS WRITTEN BY ALAN MACDONALD

Contents

CHAPTER 1

It was Thursday morning at the swimming pool. Bertie was getting changed after the lesson with Miss Crawl. His clothes lay scattered on the cubicle floor.

"HA! HA! I CAN SEE YOUR UNDERPANTS!" jeered a loud voice.

Bertie snatched up his towel. "Who said that?"

Dirty Bertie

"BERTIE'S WEARING BLUE ONES!" taunted the sing-song voice.

Bertie looked up. Two mocking eyes leered at him over the cubicle wall. It was his sworn enemy, Know-All Nick.

"Get lost!" said Bertie, throwing a sock at him.

Nick stuck out his tongue. "Make me, slowpoke!"

"Who are you calling a slowpoke?" Bertie demanded.

"You. You're always last to get changed," sneered Nick.

Bertie narrowed his eyes. "I bet I can get changed a lot quicker than you."

"Oh yeah?" said Nick.

"Yeah!" said Bertie.

"All right," said Nick. "Let's have a race."

Bertie could never resist a race,

Dirty Bertie

especially if it meant a chance to beat big-headed Nick.

"Suits me," he said. "Last one back on the bus has to sit next to Miss Boot."

Nick considered it. A smile spread slowly across his smug face.

"I've got a better idea," he said. "Last one on the bus has to come to school tomorrow in their underpants."

Bertie's jaw dropped.

Dirty Bertie

"What's the matter, slowpoke, scared you're going to lose?" sneered Nick.

Bertie glared back. "Not a chance."

"Okay, shake on it," said Nick. Bertie climbed onto the bench and the two of them shook hands.

Bertie smiled. He would show that slimy slug who was slow. Nick wouldn't see him for dust. Wait till he told his friends about this: Know-All Nick coming to school in his underpants—now that would be funny!

"Ready?" said Nick, through the wall. "Go!"

Bertie grabbed his pants and yanked them on. His fingers wrestled with his shirt buttons. Socks next.

Dirty Bertie

Where was his other sock? He wasted precious seconds hunting around the floor on his hands and knees. Who needed two socks anyway? One was plenty. He jammed on his shoes, his sweater, his coat. He stuffed his soggy trunks and towel into his bag and burst out of the cubicle.

"ARGH!" Bertie tripped over a mop and bucket that someone had left outside the door.

Dirty Bertie

In seconds he was back on his feet and racing down the corridor. "Gangway!" he yelled, barging between Donna and Pamela. "Sorry! Emergency! Can't stop!"

Eugene flattened himself against the wall as Hurricane Bertie tore past. But turning the corner, a gigantic shadow fell across his path. "BERTIE!" thundered Miss Boot. "No running in the corridor!"

"But Miss, I—"

"Walk don't run, Bertie. WALK!"

Bertie groaned. He slowed to a walk as Miss Boot watched him like a hawk to the front door. Once outside, he flew down the steps, taking them three at a time. The school bus was waiting in the parking lot. Almost there! Bertie dived through the door and flung himself into a seat.

"Yessss! I made it!" he panted. "I'm the

Dirty Bertie

first one back!"

"What took you so long, slowpoke?" drawled a jeering voice. Bertie gasped. No, it couldn't be! It wasn't possible! Know-All Nick lounged on the back seat. His hair was combed, his tie perfectly knotted and he wasn't the slightest bit out of breath.

"Tough luck, Bertie, you lose!" He smirked. "I am *so* looking forward to you coming to school tomorrow."

CHAPTER 2

Bertie sat in gloomy silence as the bus drove back to school. Darren pushed a bag of chips under his nose. "Want one?"

Bertie shook his head.

"Are you ill?" asked Darren.

"Shhh!" said Bertie. "I'm trying to think."

"What about?" Darren munched his chips noisily.

Dirty Bertie

Bertie sighed. "If I tell you, you've got to promise you won't breathe a word."

Darren leaned closer. "Okay."

Bertie looked around to check that no one could hear. He dropped his voice to a whisper. "I bet Nick I could beat him back to the bus after swimming."

"And?" said Darren.

"And I lost the bet. Now I've got to come to school in my underpants."

Darren grinned with delight. "In your underpants? HA HA HA!"

"Shut up!" hissed Bertie.

"No … but seriously…" giggled Darren, "…in your underpants? Ha ha!"

"Keep your voice down!" pleaded Bertie.

"I can't help it. That's so funny," laughed Darren.

Dirty Bertie

Eugene turned around in the seat in front. "What's so funny?"

"Bertie's going to come to school in his underpants," said Darren. "For a bet!"

Eugene stared at Bertie. "You're not?"

"No!" said Bertie, turning red. He was starting to wish he'd never mentioned it.

"But—in your underpants?"

Dirty Bertie

"Stop saying it!" cried Bertie. "You're meant to be my friends. You're meant to help me!"

Darren crunched another chip. "It's not *our* fault," he said. "You made the bet. What can we do?"

Bertie thought about it.

"I know," he said. "Do it with me!"

"What?" said Darren.

"Come to school in your underpants," said Bertie, desperately. "We'll all do it. It'll be brilliant! Why don't we?"

Darren and Eugene stared at him.

"You've got to be kidding!" said Darren. "There's no way anyone's going to see *my* underpants."

"Eugene!" pleaded Bertie. "You'll do it, won't you?"

Eugene shook his head. "Sorry, Bertie.

Dirty Bertie

I don't think my mom would let me."

Bertie slumped back in his seat and stared out the window, miserably. So much for friends. He was on his own.

Back in class, Bertie racked his brains. What was he going to do? Why oh why had he let Nick trick him into that stupid bet? He was certain that two-faced toad must have cheated. He was probably wearing half his clothes before the race even started.

In any case there was no going back now. A bet was a bet and he'd shaken on it. He tried to imagine walking into school wearing only his underpants. It didn't bear thinking about. People would be laughing at him for the next billion years.

Dirty Bertie

No, he'd just have to think of some way out.

BRIIIING! The bell sounded for recess. Bertie trudged out to the playground, lost in thought.

"Hee hee! There he is!"

Bertie turned around to see Angela Nicely and two of her little friends. Angela lived next door to Bertie. She was six years old and had been in love with Bertie ever since the time he gave her a lemon drop to stop her talking.

Dirty Bertie

"What do you want?" glared Bertie.

"Hee hee! We want to … hee hee! … ask you something!" giggled Angela.

"Not now," said Bertie. "I'm busy!" He walked faster but Angela kept up with him.

"What color are they, Bertie?" she simpered.

"Eh?" said Bertie.

"White or pink?" giggled Laura.

"Frilly or spotty?" sniggered Yasmin.

Bertie swung around to face them. "What are you talking about?"

"Your underpants!" squealed Angela. "Nick told us. You're coming to school in your underpants tomorrow!"

The girls burst into a fresh fit of giggles.

Bertie turned a deep shade of pink. "I … I'm not!" he stammered.

Dirty Bertie

Dirty Bertie

"Yes you are," said Angela. "Everybody says so."

"Listen! It's ridiculous! I'm not!" said Bertie, desperately.

Angela edged closer to him, smiling sweetly. "I'm going to bring my camera, Bertie," she trilled. "I'm going to take a picture of you in your…"

Bertie didn't wait to hear any more. He turned and fled.

He hid in the locker room, till he was sure they had gone. This was worse than he'd ever imagined. Darren and Eugene knew. So did Angela and her friends. By now the news would be around the whole school. He should have guessed that big-mouth Nick would tell everyone. Tomorrow they'd all be waiting for him—whispering and sniggering.

Dirty Bertie

If only he could think of some way out.
Bertie considered himself a master of
clever plots and cunning plans, but this
time his mind was blank. It was no use.
He wished he was a worm so he could
crawl into a hole and hide.

CHAPTER 3

"BERTIE!" boomed Miss Skinner in assembly. "Out to the front, now!"

"Me, Miss?" said Bertie.

"Yes, you. And make it snappy, I haven't got all day!"

Bertie gulped and dragged himself out to the front. Why was everyone staring at him and sniggering?

Dirty Bertie

"Haven't you forgotten something, Bertie?" said Miss Skinner.

Bertie looked down. He gasped. He was wearing nothing but his underpants.

"ARGHHHHH!" he screamed—and woke up. He breathed a sigh of relief and sank back on his pillow. Thank goodness, it was only a nightmare. But wait—what was today? Friday! Underpants Day! It wasn't a nightmare after all, it was really happening!

Dirty Bertie

There was a knock on the door. Mom came in. "Aren't you up yet, Bertie? It's time for school."

"Urrrhh!" groaned Bertie. "I don't feel well. I think I've got Germy Measles."

Mom felt his head. "Hmm," she said. "I can't see any spots."

"I think they're invisible!" he mumbled.

"Don't be silly, Bertie. There's no such thing."

"How do you know?" said Bertie. "If they're invisible they could be all over me! I could be dying of them! I could—"

"Get dressed!" said Mom. "You're going to school."

Bertie flopped out of bed. He pulled out his drawer and looked inside. All of his underpants were teeny-weeny. What he needed was extra-large ones to

Dirty Bertie

cover as much of him as possible. Wait a moment—his dad had lots of pairs of underpants. Big underpants. Surely he could borrow a pair?

Bertie tiptoed into his parents' room. He pulled open a drawer and dumped piles of underwear onto the floor. Right at the bottom he found what he was looking for. A large pair of faded blue underpants.

Bertie tried them on and looked in the mirror. They looked absurdly big, but they were the best he could find.

Dirty Bertie

Mom and Suzy were eating breakfast in the kitchen. Bertie tried to sneak past them and reach his chair.

"HA! HA!" shrieked Suzy, catching sight of him.

"What?" said Bertie. "They're only underpants."

Mom stared at him. "Good heavens, Bertie! Where are your clothes? And whose underpants are those?"

"Dad's. I just need to borrow them!" said Bertie.

"Ha ha! Hee hee!" wheezed Suzy. "You should see yourself!"

"They're way too big," said Mom. "You've got plenty of pairs of your own."

"Not like these. I need a really big pair!"

"Whatever for?"

"For a bet. I said I'd go to school in my underpants!"

"Don't be ridiculous, Bertie. You can't possibly!" said Mom.

Bertie blinked. A wave of relief swept over him. Why hadn't he thought of it before? He had promised to go to school in his underpants and he would.

Dirty Bertie

"Never mind!" he laughed. "It's okay.
Everything's okay!"

He danced out of the kitchen and
back upstairs wearing the underpants on
his head.

CHAPTER 4

Know-All Nick stood on the wall,
keeping watch along the street. It was
ten to nine and the playground was full
to bursting. Everyone had come early to
be sure of seeing Bertie's big moment.
Angela Nicely had her camera at the
ready. Darren, Donna and Eugene were
arguing about whether Bertie would

Dirty Bertie

actually go through with it. Darren said
yes. Donna said no. Eugene couldn't
make up his mind.

"Here he comes!" shouted Nick,
pointing up the street.

They all watched the entrance, eagerly.
Bertie rounded the corner and marched
in through the gates. Know-All Nick
stared in disbelief. Bertie was dressed as
normal in his sweater and jeans.

Nick jumped down from the wall and

Dirty Bertie

marched up to him.

"We had a bet!" he fumed. "You cheated! You had to come to school in your underpants!"

Bertie shrugged. "I have. I'm wearing them. Under my pants."

"Wh … wh … what?" stammered Nick, turning pale.

"What's the matter, Nick?" asked Bertie. "Don't *you* wear underpants under your pants?"

Dirty Bertie

"Of course I do," snapped Nick.

Bertie winked at Darren. "That's not what I heard. I heard you don't wear underpants."

"No," grinned Darren. "None at all."

"I do!" protested Nick.

"I heard you went without," said Bertie.

"It's not true!" wailed Nick.

"But how do we know?" said Bertie.

"Because I say so!"

"You might be lying."

"I'M NOT!" yelled Nick. "LOOK!" He pulled down his pants to prove it.

SNAP! went Angela's camera. Nick turned pink. The whole school could see his underpants and they were all laughing.

"I'll get you for this, Bertie!" he yelled.

Dirty Bertie

CHAPTER 1

Bertie flung open the door and
burst into the kitchen.

"I'd do anyfing for you, dear, anyfing!
'Cos you mean everyfing to meeeeee!"
he sang in his gruff, droning voice.

Suzy groaned. Dad covered his ears.

"Wonderful, Bertie," said Mom. "But
maybe not quite so loud."

Dirty Bertie

☆

"Miss Boot says you should sing out," said Bertie. "I was singing out."

"We heard you," said Dad. He glanced at his watch. "We'd better go or we'll be late for the audition."

"Good luck, Bertie," said Mom. "Just do your best. And try not to cause any trouble."

Bertie trooped out to the car. He didn't see what trouble you could cause just by singing. He had been looking forward to the audition ever since he'd heard his parents talking about it. Bertie's dad belonged to the Pudsley Players and every year the Players put on a show at the local theater. This year they were doing the musical, *Oliver!* Bertie had seen *Oliver!* on TV. It was about an orphan called Oliver who goes around

Dirty Bertie

asking people for more and ends up rich.
When his dad said they were looking for
children to join the cast, Bertie had
jumped at the chance. He practiced his
singing as they drove to the theater.

"I'd do anyfing…" he droned.

"Bertie!" sighed Dad.

"What? I'm only singing."

"Well don't! You'll cause an accident.
And at least try to keep to the tune."

Dirty Bertie

"I am keeping to the tune!" said Bertie. "That's how it goes... 'I'd do ANYFING...!'"

"BERTIE!" shouted Dad, gripping the steering wheel.

Bertie lapsed into silence. The trouble with some people, he thought, was they just didn't appreciate good singing.

At the theater he found the dressing room crowded with eager children waiting to be called on stage. Bertie elbowed his way through the crowd and found an empty seat next to a pale boy wearing a large brown cap. It was only when the boy looked up and scowled that he recognized his old enemy, Know-All Nick.

40

Dirty Bertie

"What are you doing here?" sneered Nick.

"What are *you* doing here?" replied Bertie.

"If you must know I'm going to be in the play," boasted Nick.

"Well so am I," said Bertie.

"Huh!" scoffed Nick. "They're not that desperate. Anyway, Miss Lavish only wants five boys. You don't stand a chance."

"Who's Miss Lavish?" asked Bertie.

"Don't you know? She's the director." Nick removed his cap and smoothed back his hair. "Anyway which part do you want?"

"The Artful Dodger," said Bertie.

Nick snorted. "Sorry, that part's taken. I'm going to be Dodger."

Dirty Bertie

"Liar," said Bertie. "She hasn't even heard you sing yet."

Nick gave him a smug look. "That's what you think."

A woman with a clipboard poked her head around the door.

"Nicholas?" she said. "Miss Lavish is

Dirty Bertie

ready for you now."

Know-All Nick pulled on his cap and
went to the door. "Oh by the way,
Bertie," he said. "Miss Lavish has heard me
sing lots of times. She's my godmother."
He stuck out his tongue and vanished
through the door.

CHAPTER 2

Bertie sat in the dressing room waiting to be called. He would show that sneaky slimeball, Nick. His audition would be so good Miss Lavish would fall on her knees and beg him to play the Artful Dodger. The room started to empty slowly as, one by one, the other children were called on stage. An hour went by.

Dirty Bertie

Bertie was the only one left in the dressing room.

"Bertie?" said the lady with the clipboard. "Miss Lavish will see you now. And please don't pick your nose." Bertie removed his finger. He bet the Artful Dodger picked his nose all the time.

Bertie stood in the middle of the stage and squinted into the spotlights. He'd never been on a stage before and he'd certainly never been asked to sing a solo. Miss Lavish sat a few rows back, scribbling notes. She was a large woman wrapped in a scarlet shawl. Bertie coughed nervously. Miss Lavish looked up.

"Hello dear. And you are?"

Dirty Bertie

"Bertie," said Bertie.

"Great. And what are you going to sing for us?"

"Oh um … 'I'd do Anyfing'. It's from *Oliver!*" said Bertie.

Dirty Bertie

"I know where it's from, dear," said Miss Lavish, peering over her glasses. She raised a plump finger. "Come in with the piano then."

Miss Plunk played the opening bars on the piano. Bertie turned and walked off stage.

"Where are you going now?" cried Miss Lavish. "Come back!"

"You said to come in with the piano," said Bertie. "I can't come in if I'm still here."

"I meant come in singing. Come in with the music!"

"Oh," said Bertie. He wished she'd say what she meant.

Miss Lavish nodded wearily at Miss Plunk. "Let's try again, shall we?"

The piano played. Bertie took a deep

breath and opened his mouth. To his horror he realized that the words had gone clean out of his head. He had practiced them a million times but his mind was a total blank. He began anyway, hoping the words would come back to him.

"I'd um … anyfing … um … you …
um … anyfing! 'Cos you um … anyfing!
… um er …"

Miss Lavish's mouth had fallen open.
Whatever Bertie was singing it wasn't a
tune. She raised a hand to put a stop to
the awful dirge, but Bertie ploughed on,
bellowing any word he could remember.

Dirty Bertie

"I'd … er … ANYFING! And you'd um … ANYFING!"

"Stop!" begged Miss Lavish, waving her hands. "Stop, stop, STOP!"

Bertie stopped. He waited for Miss Lavish to start clapping. True, he had missed out one or two of the words, but no one could say he hadn't sung out. He bet no one else had sung out quite as well as he had. Miss Lavish took off her glasses.

"Thank you, Billy, that was ah … lovely. But I'm afraid I have all the children I need."

Bertie blinked. "Oh."

"But thank you so much for coming."

Bertie sniffed and wiped his nose. "You don't want me to be the Artful Dodger?" he asked.

Dirty Bertie

Miss Lavish shook her head. "No, dear, we have our Dodger already."

Know-All Nick waved to Bertie from behind the stage curtain, with a "told-you-so" smile on his face.

"I could sing something else," offered Bertie. "I know lots of songs."

"No, no more, please," said Miss Lavish hastily. "Run along now."

Bertie dug his hands in his pockets and trailed off.

Miss Lavish's assistant leaned over and whispered something in her ear.

"Wait one moment, dear!" she called. Bertie was back in an instant.

"I gather there is one very small part we have yet to cast," said Miss Lavish.

"Yes?" said Bertie.

"Well, what we really need is a dog."

Dirty Bertie

"A dog?" said Bertie.

"Yes, the costume's rather small but you look about the right size. What do you think?"

"Me?" said Bertie. "Play a dog?"

"Yes. If you wouldn't mind?"

Mind? Bertie's eyes shone. It was a dream come true!

CHAPTER 3

Mom was waiting for them when they got home.

"Well? How did it go?" she asked.

Bertie took off his coat. "Great. I got the part," he said.

"Really? They want you to be the Artful Dodger?"

"No, better than that. They want me

Dirty Bertie

to be the dog," said Bertie.

"The dog?" Mom turned to Dad.
"What dog?"

"It seems Mr. Dodds needs a dog. He's
playing Bill Sykes," explained Dad. "And
they asked Bertie to do it."

"I get a costume and everything," said
Bertie. "Miss Lavish says I ought to start
practicing right away." He padded past
them on all fours and picked up
Whiffer's bowl in his mouth. He dropped
it at Mom's feet and began to whine.

Dirty Bertie

Mom looked at Dad. "How many weeks do we have of this?"

"Ten," sighed Dad. "Look at it this way, at least he won't be singing."

Over the next ten weeks, Bertie went to rehearsals with his dad. His part turned out to be less exciting than he had hoped. Most of the time he had to trot after Mr. Dodds or sit quietly while the other actors talked on and on. His big moment came in the final act when he dashed to the front of the stage and barked to bring the police running. Bertie practiced that one "Woof!" a hundred different ways, but he couldn't help feeling his talents were going to waste.

Dirty Bertie

In rehearsals he tried to add in a few "doggy touches" to liven up the dull bits of the play. Whenever Know-All Nick came on stage, Bertie bared his teeth and growled fiercely. But Miss Lavish said his growling was drowning out the words and could he please keep quiet. Bertie took to scratching his ear with his paw. But Miss Lavish said he was "destroying the atmosphere" and could he please keep still.

The following week, Bertie thought he could smell a cat and went sniffing

around the stage. Miss Lavish lost her
temper and threw down her script.
Bertie sighed. He didn't see how he was
meant to play a dog that didn't growl,
scratch or even sniff. He might as well be
a goldfish! To make matters worse, there
was still no sign of his costume. Bertie
didn't have a chance to try it on until
the dress rehearsal. It was an itchy
brown suit. The head had floppy ears
attached and was three sizes too small.
Bertie complained to Miss Lavish but she
said she didn't have time for silly details.

CHAPTER 4

Finally the big night arrived. There was a buzz of excitement as Mom and Suzy took their seats and the lights went down. The curtain drew back to reveal the painted streets of London Town.

Backstage, Bertie was still in the dressing room. "Hurry up! We're starting!" said Nick, pulling on his jacket.

Dirty Bertie

"It's this head!" moaned Bertie. "It's got smaller. I can't get it on!"

"Oh give it here!" said Nick, impatiently. He grabbed the dog's head and jammed it down hard over Bertie.

"Mmmnff!" said Bertie in a muffled voice. "That's the wrong way around! I can't see!"

Nick wasn't listening. He had hurried out of the door, anxious not to miss his cue. Bertie tried to twist the dog head back around, but it was jammed on tight and wouldn't budge.

Dirty Bertie

Mom and Suzy clapped as the first act came to an end

"Where's Bertie?" whispered Suzy. "I haven't seen him yet."

"Shhh!" replied Mom. "This is his big entrance."

Mr. Dodds entered as Bill Sykes, making his way to Fagin's hideout. He looked around for his faithful dog, Bullseye, but there was no sign of him.

"Bertie!" he hissed. "Bertie!"

Backstage Dad looked around. "Where's Bertie? He should be on stage!"

At that moment, Bertie stumbled up the steps, still wrestling with his head.

"You're meant to be on," Dad hissed. He grabbed Bertie by the arm and shoved him on stage. There were giggles from the audience.

"What's he doing?" whispered Suzy.

"Oh dear," said Mom. "I think he's got his head on back to front."

Mr. Dodds took hold of Bullseye's head and tried to twist it around. The audience roared with laughter.

☆

"Ow!" said Bertie loudly. "That hurts!"

Mr. Dodds was sweating. "Shhh!" he muttered, thrusting Bertie behind a lamp-post where he couldn't do any harm. "Stay!" he commanded.

Sykes and Fagin started an argument but no one was paying much attention. They were all watching Bullseye. Bertie was rolling around on the ground, tugging at his head with both hands.

"Is this part of the story?" whispered Suzy.

"I'm not sure," replied Mom. "I don't remember it in the film."

Watching from the wings, Miss Lavish ground her teeth. At this rate Bertie would ruin everything!

"Miss Plunk!" she hissed. "Miss Plunk! Start the next song."

Dirty Bertie

Miss Plunk thumped on the piano. Fagin sang "You've got to pick a pocket or two" and Dodger and his gang began to dance.

"Bertie! Get off!" urged Dad. Bertie trotted blindly in the wrong direction— straight toward the dancers who were whirling faster and faster.

Know-All Nick took a step back, tripped over Bertie, and tumbled straight into an apple cart. Apples spilled across the stage and under the dancers' feet. Miss Lavish watched in horror as Mr. Dodds stumbled into a lamp-post and sent it crashing down on the streets of London. The tall scenery swayed dangerously.

"Look out!" shouted Dad. "It's going to fall!"

Dirty Bertie

"Arghhhh!" screamed the actors, running in all directions.

"What's happening?" asked Bertie, left alone on stage.

CRASH! went the scenery as it came tumbling down.

There was a hushed silence. The audience waited to see if this was the end of the show. Slowly the dust cleared to reveal a mound of broken scenery.

Dirty Bertie

A door moved. From underneath it, Bertie scrambled out. He tugged at his dog's head and finally managed to pull it off. Puzzled, he looked around. *Where had everybody gone?* The audience were all staring at him in astonishment. Bertie suddenly remembered he hadn't given his one and only line.

Dirty Bertie

"WOOF!" he barked.

The audience laughed and clapped and cheered. Bertie grinned and gave a low bow. He was still bowing when Dad brought the curtain down.

Dirty Bertie

Turning around, he saw Miss Lavish, Mr. Dodds and the rest of the cast advancing on him. Their hair was white with dust and their faces were grim.

"You wait," said Miss Lavish. "You just wait…"

But Bertie didn't wait. He did what any dog would do—he took to his heels and ran.

AVAST THERE ME HEARTIES!

Come to Black-Eyed
Bertie's Pirate Party

Saturday 2 pm

Dress as a pirate

P.S. ~ Bring me a present or
Walk ye plank!

CHAPTER 1

Bertie could hardly wait—he'd been
counting down the days to his birthday
for weeks and now it was almost here.
It was going to be the best party ever.
Bertie already had his pirate captain's
hat and plastic eyepatch. All he had
to do now was hand out invitations to
his friends.

Dirty Bertie

"A pirate party? Great!" said Darren. "When is it?"

"Saturday afternoon," said Bertie.

"Not this Saturday?"

"Yes!"

Darren's face fell. "But I'm going to Royston's party!"

"Royston's?" Bertie couldn't believe his ears. Royston Rich was the biggest show-off in the school and no one in Bertie's class liked him. "But you hate Royston!"

Dirty Bertie

"I know but he's having a swimming party. He's got a pool in his backyard with a wave machine and everything!"

"But what about my party?"

Darren shrugged. "Sorry, Bertie. Royston gave out his invitations last week. Didn't you get one?"

Bertie hadn't. Not that he cared. Who wanted to go to Royston's rubbish party? He crossed Darren's name off his list. Still, if Darren let him down at least he could rely on Eugene…

"Saturday?" asked Eugene.

"Yes. You're coming, aren't you?"

Eugene turned pink. "I'd like to but I'm going to Royston's party."

"Not you as well!"

"Sorry, Bertie. He's got his own swimming pool with a—"

"I know! A wave machine and everything!" scowled Bertie.

"Yes and did he tell you about the inflatables? It's going to be brilliant. Everyone's going…" Eugene went pinker still. "Oh—aren't you, Bertie?"

"No!" snapped Bertie. "I'm having my own party and it'll be a billion times better than his."

Scratch! Bertie crossed Eugene off his list. At recess he gave Donna her invitation. Scratch! She was going to Royston's party too. So were Alex, Dan, Stan, Sunil, and Pamela. At the end of the day the only invitation left was for Angela Nicely. Bertie hadn't wanted to invite her in the first place—he'd only included Angela because he'd gone to her party. Scratch! Out went Angela.

Dirty Bertie

That left—Bertie looked at his list—
no one at all. *Well, see if I care*, thought
Bertie. *I'll have a great party on my own.
Loads more cake and chips for me!*
Hang on though, if no one came to his
party he wouldn't get any presents. And
playing pirates wasn't much fun when
the only enemy was Whiffer.

CHAPTER 2

Bertie slammed the front door. He flung down his bag and clumped upstairs to his room. A minute later, Mom poked her head around the door.

"Bertie, are you all right? How was school today?"

"Terrible," grumbled Bertie. "No one's coming to my party."

Dirty Bertie

"No one? Didn't you give out the invitations?"

Bertie explained about Royston Rich's swimming party.

"Oh dear!" said Mom. "Fancy it being on the same day as yours! Maybe we should move your party to next weekend?"

"That's years away!" moaned Bertie. "If anyone should move I don't see why it should be me. Why doesn't he move his smelly old party?"

His mom sighed. "Bertie, things don't always work out the way you want."

"Huh!" said Bertie, bitterly. "I bet if we had a swimming pool everyone would come to my party. Why can't we get a swimming pool in *our* backyard?"

His mom gave him one of her looks and closed the door.

Bertie lay on his bed. It wasn't fair.
Who did Royston think he was pinching
all Bertie's friends? Just because he didn't
have any friends of his own! Well Black-
Eyed Bertie, the scourge of the seven
seas, wasn't beaten yet. If Royston was
boasting about his super swimming pool,
he would just have to think of something
better. He racked his brains. What did
pirates do when they weren't swabbing

decks or splicing the mainbrace?
Of course—they hunted for buried
treasure!

Bertie tiptoed into his parents' room.
He went straight to the present drawer
where his mom kept anything she didn't
want him to see. Inside he found party
hats, balloons—and a big bag of
chocolate coins. "Ahaar!" cried Bertie.
"Gold doubloons!"

Dirty Bertie

Out in the backyard he dug a hole
and carefully slipped in the bag of coins.
He was just smoothing over the earth
when he heard a ring at the door.

It was Royston Rich.

"Oh hello, Bertie," said Royston,
carelessly. "I brought your invitation."

Bertie stared in surprise. "You're inviting
me?"

Royston shrugged. "Andrew can't
come so I suppose you might as well.
I couldn't think of anyone else."

"Well I can't come either, I'm having
my own party," said Bertie.

"I know, but no one's going to yours,
are they?" gloated Royston.

"Huh, that's what you think! Loads of
people are coming."

"Yeah? Like who?"

"Like … loads of people."

"Well everyone from our class is going to be at *my* party," boasted Royston. He pushed the invitation under Bertie's nose. "Keep it anyway, in case you change your mind."

Bertie snatched it off him. "I won't," he said.

"Suit yourself," said Royston. "You'll be missing the best party of the year. We're having a wave—"

Dirty Bertie

SLAM! Bertie shut the door in his face.

He turned around to find Mom barring his way.

"Bertie, someone's been nosing in the present drawer."

"Oh. Have they?" said Bertie, innocently.

"Yes and a bag of chocolate coins is missing. I bought them as prizes for your party. Do you know anything about that?"

Dirty Bertie

"Erm…" said Bertie.

"Bertie, if I find out you've eaten them…"

"I haven't!"

"Good, then you can give them back. Right now."

"But Mom, I need them for the treasure hunt! You can't have a pirate party without buried treasure."

Mom put a hand to her head. "Buried treasure? Bertie you haven't!"

"What?"

"Buried them?"

"Well, I might have," said Bertie. "But it's okay, I know exactly where they are!"

"Where?" demanded Mom.

"Um … somewhere in the backyard."

CHAPTER 3

Saturday afternoon came. Bertie stood at the living room window staring along the street. He was dressed in his pirate hat and eyepatch. Whiffer, his faithful sea dog, sat at his side keeping watch.

It was half past two.

His mom came and joined him at the window. "I'm sorry, Bertie, I don't think

Dirty Bertie

anyone's coming. Why don't you go to Royston's party? It's not too late."

"I don't want to!" glared Bertie.

"I'm sure you'll have fun," said Mom.

"I won't. I hate swimming!"

"Don't be silly, Bertie. All your friends will be there."

"Huh!" scowled Bertie. "I haven't got any friends."

Mom sighed. "Look, we'll have your party another day. Why don't you just go and enjoy yourself?"

"All right, all right!" said Bertie. "As long as Whiffer can come too."

Mom frowned. "It's a swimming party, Bertie, dogs aren't invited."

"Then I'm not going," said Bertie stubbornly. "If Whiffer can't go then I'm not going either."

Dirty Bertie

Ten minutes later they arrived at Royston's big house on Poshley Drive. Bertie's mom buzzed the intercom at the gates.

"Do come through!" sang Mrs. Rich's voice. "We're in the pool!"

The gates swung slowly open and Bertie trudged through with Whiffer at his heels. Screams and laughter came from the enormous swimming pool in the backyard.

"Hi Bertie!" waved Darren, zooming down the slide and landing with a splash.

Royston looked up. "Oh hello, Bertie! I thought you were too busy to come?"

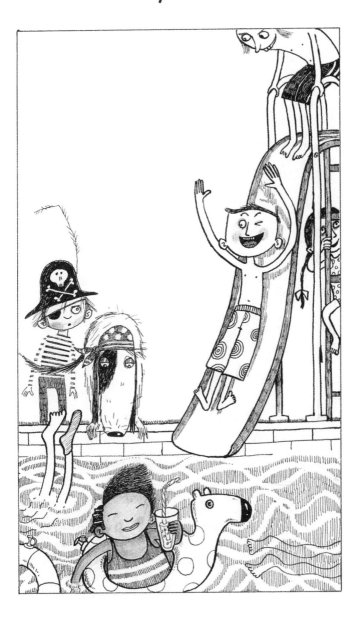

Dirty Bertie

"I can't stay long," said Bertie, looking at his watch. "I've got people waiting."

"What do you think of my swimming pool? Super isn't it?"

Bertie shrugged. "It's all right."

"You better get changed. We're just about to start the wave machine!"

Bertie wandered over to the barbecue where Mr. Rich was cooking hot dogs and enormous steaks. Whiffer's nose twitched at the smell of sausages.

"Hey!" shouted Mr. Rich.

Bertie looked up. "Me?"

"Yes, you. Is that your dog?"

Bertie glanced down at Whiffer who was sniffing the meat. "He likes sausages."

"I don't care what he likes, take him somewhere else and tie him up. I don't want him near the food!"

Dirty Bertie

Bertie dragged Whiffer away and tied
him to a post on the lawn tennis court.
"Sorry, Whiffer," said Bertie. "You stay
there and I'll get you something to eat!"

Whiffer whined and pulled at his leash.

"Sit!" commanded Bertie. "Sit!" Whiffer
sniffed around then squatted down on
his hind legs. Uh-oh—that could
only mean one thing.
Bertie glanced
around, hoping
no one had noticed.
It was lucky he'd
remembered to bring
along his pooper-
scooper just in case. He
scooped the lump of poop
into a small plastic bag. Now where to
get rid of it?

Dirty Bertie

He wandered back to the house,
holding the bag at arm's length. By the
pool he almost bumped into Mrs. Rich
carrying a tray of lemonade. Mrs. Rich
stopped and stared at the bag in Bertie's
hand. She looked closer. Was that…?
Good heavens! It was! She gasped.

"It's all right, it's only dog poo," said
Bertie, holding the bag up for inspection.

Dirty Bertie

"Ugh! Take it away!" cried Mrs. Rich.

"I am taking it away," said Bertie. "But I'm looking for a trash can."

"By the back door!" Mrs. Rich flapped a hand. "Take it away before you drop it!"

Bertie walked on. He didn't see why Royston's mom was making such a big fuss. After all, dogs had to poo just like everyone else. And he'd been to a lot of trouble clearing it up—you would have thought she'd be grateful!

He was so busy grumbling to himself that he didn't notice the paper plate of raspberry jello lying right in his path. Bertie stepped in the jello and slipped. "Woaaaaaahhh!" He lost his balance and the bag slipped from his grasp. It sailed into the air and the lump of poop shot out like a torpedo.

Dirty Bertie

Up, up, up it rose…

Then down, down, down—landing in the swimming pool with a loud PLOP!

"Uh-oh," said Bertie.

CHAPTER 4

Royston zoomed down the slide, landing in the deep end with a great splash. He came up spluttering for air. What was that floating in the water? Something brown like a leaf.

"ARGGHHHH!" he shrieked. "A POOP! THERE'S A POOP IN THE POOL!"

Bertie had never dreamed one little piece of doggy-do could cause so much panic. Thirty children scrambled to get out of the pool, screaming as if a killer shark was after them.

"Do something!" cried Mrs. Rich to her husband.

Mr. Rich fetched a net and fished around in the deep end. But the poop had sunk to the bottom and didn't want to be caught.

"Don't worry," said Royston. "My dad'll
sort it out. Then we can all go back in."

"Eeugh!" Donna pulled a face. "I'm not
going in there!"

"Nor me," said Pamela. "It's full of
pooey germs."

"It's yucky!"

"It's smelly!"

"But what about the party?" asked
Eugene. "What are we going to do?"

Bertie pulled on his eyepatch and
leaped onto a sunlounger.

"Who wants to come back to my
house for a pirate party?" he cried.

"Can we have sword fights?" asked
Darren.

"Of course!" nodded Bertie. "And
walking the plank. And a treasure hunt—
with real chocolate coins!"

Dirty Bertie

"Chocolate? Why didn't you say so before?" said Darren. "Come on!"

Thirty children charged out of the gates and down the street with Black-Eyed Bertie leading the way. It was going to be a brilliant birthday after all, he thought, and all thanks to Whiffer and his pongy present!